THE
VANISHED
ONE

ANNE SCHRAFF

STANDING TALL MYSTERIES
BY ANNE SCHRAFF

Project Editor: Carol E. Newell
Cover Designer and Illustrator: TSA design group

© 1995 Saddleback Publishing, Inc.

SADDLEBACK
PUBLISHING • INC.

3505 Cadillac Ave., Building F-9
Costa Mesa, CA 92626

ISBN 1-56254-159-5
Printed in the United States of America
03 02 01 M 99 98 97 96   8 7 6 5 4 3 2 1

Chapter 1

"Hey," Matt Nuanes yelled, "she's not here!"

Justin Alvarez dropped his books on his desk. He looked up at the empty desk where Ms. Adriana Sanchez taught Algebra. He was disappointed. He was anxious to get that last test back, and now there would be a substitute teacher. Justin thought he just might have pulled an A, his first A, on that last test.

"Sanchez gone?" a boy shouted. "All right! I didn't get my homework done last night!"

"She's never absent. She must be really sick," Justin said. Ms. Sanchez was the best freshman math teacher Lincoln-

Juarez High ever had. Everybody—even kids who didn't like her—had to admit she was good. Justin's worst subject was always math, and he dreaded Algebra. Somehow Ms. Sanchez made all those numbers and letters make sense to Justin and most of his classmates.

A middle-aged man marched into class right before the bell. "I'm Mr. Tremayne. I'll be teaching Algebra today," he said.

"Where's Ms. Sanchez?" Justin asked.

"Oh, I have no idea," Mr. Tremayne said with a wry grin. "You know they don't tell substitute teachers anything."

After class, Justin went to the school office. "I'm wondering about Ms. Sanchez," Justin asked a gray-haired clerk. "Will she be back tomorrow?"

"We aren't sure," the woman said crisply. Maybe it was just Justin's imagination, but he was sure she looked suspicious, as if there was something strange about Ms. Sanchez not being in school.

"See," Justin persisted, "if she was really sick or something, I'd like to send her a card."

The clerk looked at Justin as if he was crazy. Most of the people at this school were like that. They were like robots. They thought you were crazy if you showed emotion. Ms. Sanchez wasn't like that though. She was wonderfully human. She laughed and yelled, and she made sure everybody— even the slow kids—could do basic Algebra. Before he got into her class, Justin never made better than a C in math. Now he was getting Bs. "You will have a substitute teacher as long as necessary," the clerk said.

As Justin was walking away, he heard the clerk say to another woman in the office, "It's not like her to not even call in. She's usually so responsible. We're lucky there was a sub on campus for another period."

The younger woman laughed. "Maybe she eloped with her boyfriend. This younger generation is kind of flaky. I know. I am one of them!"

Justin stiffened. How dare they talk about Ms. Sanchez as if she were some irresponsible fool? Sure, she had a boy-friend. She was only about twenty-five. A guy in a red sports car picked her up a few times. But she wouldn't just run off with him and leave her class in the lurch. She put her heart and soul into teaching Algebra, and she took a lot of pride in her success.

As Justin passed the snack machine, his friend Michelle Navarro said, "Not buying anything, Justin?"

"I'm worried about Ms. Sanchez, Michelle. They're acting weird in the office like they don't know where she is. I mean, she didn't even call in or anything. That's not like her," Justin said.

Michelle put her hand on Justin's arm. "You really like her, don't you?" she said.

"Yeah, like before I got in her class I felt so stupid. I figured I'd never in a million years crack math. Everybody in my family is smart but me ... Ms. Sanchez gave me the key to being smart, too!" Justin said.

"Maybe she was in an auto accident," Michelle gasped. "Maybe she hasn't had the chance to call in."

Chapter 2

Justin turned on the radio station that featured traffic updates. If any bad accident was tying up the roads they'd be talking about it. But they were saying everything was running smoothly.

At lunchtime, Justin returned to the office. He saw another teacher, Ms. Bracamonte, who sometimes ate lunch with Ms. Sanchez. She was taking something into the office. "Ms. Bracamonte," Justin said, "have you heard what happened to Ms. Sanchez? Did she call in yet?"

Ms. Bracamonte taught History. She was okay, but nothing special, at least not from Justin's viewpoint. She just did her job and hoped everybody caught on. "I'm sure everything is under control, Justin," Ms. Bracamonte said. "Nothing for you students to worry about."

Justin felt his anger rise. "I bet if you knew something awful happened to Ms. Sanchez you wouldn't even say," Justin snapped. "You teachers figure kids don't have the right to know anything because we're kids."

Ms. Bracamonte gave Justin a cold stare. "You're being rude, Justin. I'm sure you don't mean to be. I don't appreciate your tone of voice," she said.

"I'd just like to know what happened to a teacher I happen to care about, Ms. Bracamonte," Justin said. "If that's rude, I'm sorry!"

Ms. Bracamonte's cold stare frosted over. "I'm sure you have a class to go to, Justin, and I have better things to do than to stand here gossiping with a freshman about a vanished teacher!"

Vanished? Is that what she was, vanished?

Justin barely listened to anything in class for the rest of the day. He couldn't wait for the last bell. He jumped on his motorcycle and drove four miles to where Ms. Sanchez lived. Justin knew where she lived because she'd invited all the kids competing in the math tournament there. Twelve kids were crammed into her white stucco house. Ms. Sanchez delighted everybody by serving homemade *empanadas*, biscuit dough filled with chopped meat then deep fried.

Justin pulled into the driveway and parked. He stared at the bright poinsettias around the door. Kids were always giving Ms. Sanchez poinsettias for Christmas, and she planted them. Justin gave her one too, last Christmas, with *Feliz Navidad* printed on the card.

Nobody answered when Justin rang the doorbell. The shades were drawn in every window. The little house seemed to shriek the absence of Ms. Sanchez, as if she'd been gone a long time and would never be coming home.

Justin had a cat once, a black and white Tom. One day he didn't come to be fed, and Justin looked all over the neighborhood for him in vain. The whole yard looked forlorn and lonely because the cat was gone. Justin had a cold feeling right away that his cat was gone for good, and it was true. Now he felt that way about Ms. Sanchez. Something truly terrible had happened, and she wouldn't be coming back.

Justin was nearly overwhelmed by a sense of sadness. Ms. Sanchez wouldn't return to Room 212 again to write algebraic equations on the board. She'd never march to the board on her purple high heels and talk about positive and negative numbers in her bright, animated voice.

Justin went to the green stucco house next door and rang the doorbell.

He asked the elderly woman who answered about Ms. Sanchez. The woman shook her head vigorously. No, she saw nothing. Justin scribbled his name and phone number on a paper and handed it to her. Then she quickly closed and locked the door. Maybe later she'd remember something and call Justin. Maybe. But he didn't think so.

Chapter 3

Justin tried the house on the other side, but nobody was home. Then he went home.

"Oh, Justin," Mom said when he told her about Ms. Sanchez being missing, "you're making too much of this. She's a young, pretty woman. Maybe she and her boyfriend had a fight. Now they're off somewhere trying to make up."

Dad laughed. "I'll bet she ran away to get married. Probably didn't want all the hassle of a big wedding," he said.

Mom gave Dad a playful shove. "You! You wanted us to do that. Justin, imagine! Your father wanted us to elope after all my dreams about wearing my mother's beautiful satin embroidered dress with the long lace train. I had the bouquet to give to Our Lady of Guadalupe and everything, and he wanted to elope!"

"Ay," Dad laughed, "so much *tumulto*! I'll bet your math teacher and her fella just took off and got married, Justin. She's probably forgotten all about her job by now."

"Dad," Justin said irritably, "you don't know Ms. Sanchez. She takes her work seriously."

"More seriously than *amor*? I don't think so, Justin. Algebra is not as important as *amor*!"

Justin went to his room, disgusted at how lightly his parents were taking Ms. Sanchez's disappearance. He opened his Algebra book and started his homework. Ms. Sanchez collected it every day. Students got marked down if they didn't turn it in. Then, suddenly, Justin slammed his book shut. Ms.

Sanchez wouldn't be there tomorrow. Nobody had told him that, but he knew it was true. And Mr. Tremayne wouldn't care if the homework was done or not.

Justin tried to think of someone who would know where Ms. Sanchez had gone. He remembered she had a cousin, Sandi Garcia, who was a student at Lincoln-Juarez. She might know something. Maybe at least she'd know the names and addresses of other relatives.

Justin found Sandi's phone number in a school directory. She was the president of the Red Cross club. "Hey, Sandi, this is Justin Alvarez. I'm in your cousin's Algebra class, and I'm worried about where she is …"

"Yeah, I'm worried, too," Sandi interrupted.

"Well … uh … do you know where her parents live?" Justin asked.

"Somewhere deep in Mexico. Some little village. She has no relatives around here, except us," Sandi said.

"What about her boyfriend?" Justin asked. "I've never seen him close, but he drives a red sports car. Do you know his name, Sandi?"

"Just that she calls him Dave. They weren't all that serious, Justin. We can't imagine what happened. If she doesn't show up tomorrow, we're going to call the police," Sandi said.

"I think you had better call them now," Justin said. "I mean, what if she's ... uh ... in that house and hurt or something?"

Sandi's mother came to the phone. "I'm Adriana's aunt. Sandi says you think something is really wrong. My husband is out of town on business. If you'd meet us over at Adriana's house, we could all go in together and look around ... you know."

"You bet," Justin said.

Justin ran outside to his motorcycle and headed for Ms. Sanchez's house.

Sandi and her mother arrived about five minutes after Justin. Mrs. Garcia was a tiny woman who looked a little bit like Ms. Sanchez. She seemed very nervous. She waved a key in the air and said, "Adriana gave me this key when she went on vacation last year so I could water her plants. I feel very frightened to be going into the house now."

Justin's legs felt numb. He was frightened, too. What if Ms. Sanchez was in there ... what if she was lying somewhere hurt or worse. "We'd better go in," he told Mrs. Garcia. Then he steeled himself for the worst.

Chapter 4

The door swung open and Mrs. Garcia and Sandi stepped aside so Justin could go in first. They made it clear that was how they wanted it. Justin was only a high school freshman, but he was six feet tall and weighed one hundred sixty pounds. He looked like a man.

It was dark inside the living room. Justin flipped on a switch and glanced around. He half expected to see overturned lamps and broken vases where an intruder had rummaged for valuables. But everything looked in place. The beautiful watercolors Ms. Sanchez painted of her beloved Mexican village hung on the walls. The yellow roses, still fresh and fragrant from her garden looked beautiful in a creamy vase.

"We better look in the bedroom," Justin said. Maybe Ms. Sanchez had gotten sick in the night and died in her bed. Last year that happened to a basketball player at Lincoln-Juarez. Life always hangs by a thread. That's what Justin's grandfather often said.

Justin felt scared and awkward to be going into Ms. Sanchez's bedroom like this.

"See anything, Justin?" Sandi asked in a high-pitched voice behind him. If it was something bad, she didn't want to see it at all.

"Room's empty," Justin said with relief. The bed was made with a pretty chenille bedspread tucked in and a small, stuffed cat perched on the pillow. Everything was neat and orderly, like Ms. Sanchez's desk at school. There was no sign of a struggle, nothing unusual.

"Well, it's as if she locked up and

just went away," Mrs. Garcia said.

Sandi looked around the room. "There's her appointment book on the table by the bed ..."

Justin picked up the leather-bound book that sat on top of a neat pile of corrected Algebra tests. It was just as he thought. She'd finished the tests and would have passed them out this morning. Justin read aloud, "Ezekiel 33, 7-9, Romans 13, 8-10 ..."

"That must be for Sunday. She reads at the 9:30 mass," Sandi explained. "What does she say for today?"

"Take tests to school,..." Justin read, "and then Dave, 8:30 P.M. She must have an appointment with this guy for tonight."

"Look," Sandi said, flipping through the corrected tests, "you got an A, Justin."

That news would have ordinarily made Justin's day, but now it left him empty and unmoved. "Don't mess with her stuff, Sandi," Justin said almost harshly. "Look, I bet this guy, Dave, showed up early for the date. Somebody has got to know who he is."

"Here's an address book," Mrs. Garcia said.

Justin flipped through the many names and addresses. "Hey," Justin said, "some pages have been ripped out … I to L is gone."

"That's odd," Mrs. Garcia said.

Justin tried to picture it. Dave came last night. He didn't want to wait for tonight. He talked Ms. Sanchez into leaving with him, but before they left he ripped his own name from the address book. That meant he didn't want anybody to know who he was.

Why would he do that? Justin turned to Mrs. Garcia, "There's no Dave in her book, so his last name must start with an I, J, K, or L. He must be on one of the pages he ripped out."

"Justin, aren't you jumping to conclusions?" Mrs. Garcia asked. "Maybe they had a fight and Adriana ripped out the pages in anger so she wouldn't be reminded of him."

"You have to call the police, Mrs. Garcia," Justin said. "We've waited too long already."

Chapter 5

The police weren't eager to put a lot of time into searching for Ms. Sanchez. She was, after all, a twenty-five year old woman, and there was no sign of foul play. Even her little silver car sat untouched in the garage.

"People are unpredictable," Lt. Wong said. "You think they are reliable and the next thing you know they are skiing in Aspen, and they forgot to tell their loved ones or their boss."

Even Justin's friend, Michelle, went along with the theory that Ms. Sanchez had done something impulsive, probably with Dave. "Maybe she went to Hawaii. Or maybe she went home to her little village in Mexico. Maybe she took Dave to Mexico to meet her parents."

"That is so stupid," Justin stormed. "Somebody like Ms. Sanchez would not just drop her good job and go skipping off to Mexico on a lark!"

"Oh, Justin," Michelle snapped, "you've made an idol of her. She's only a human being. She fell madly in love, and she's gone a little crazy. Now she and Dave are running barefoot in the surf somewhere in Mexico near some lovely tropical village. Justin, do you think dull old Algebra is her whole life?"

"That guy, Dave, he ripped his name from her address book. I know it! He did something to her, and he doesn't want anybody to know who he is," Justin said.

"Justin," Michelle said, "Lt. Wong said the school is getting in touch with Ms. Sanchez's parents. Probably that will settle everything."

Justin headed for Room 212 after school that day. Ms. Sanchez would always stay late in case a student needed some extra help. But Mr. Tremayne headed for the faculty lounge after the last bell. He left the room open, and Justin walked in. He looked around to make sure nobody was watching. Then he went to Ms. Sanchez's desk, sliding the drawer open. He saw student homework and late slips and also a birthday card. He snatched it up and read it. *Dear Adriana*, began the written salutation, *Let's celebrate at Caleb's Chop House, our "favorite" place! Ha ha ha! Love, Dave.*

Mr. Tremayne was coming in and Justin returned the card. "Hi, Mr. Tremayne," Justin said. "I was just ... you know ... wondering if Ms. Sanchez came back," he said.

Mr. Tremayne laughed. "Not likely. The principal is really ticked off. She's AWOL, you know. It looks like I've stumbled on a long term sub assignment."

Justin went outside, his head spinning. Caleb's Chop House must have been their favorite haunt. Maybe the people there would know who Dave was. Justin ran to his motorcycle and drove the three miles to Caleb's, a plain-looking place in the mall. He went inside and stopped the first waitress he saw. "Hey, excuse me, but I'm looking for a guy named Dave who comes here a lot," he said.

The waitress laughed. "The world is full of Daves. Our cook is a Dave, my brother-in-law is a Dave, and once I even dated a Dave."

"He used to come in here with a woman named Adriana, a real pretty lady," Justin said.

"Hey, Pablo," the waitress shouted to a boy, "do you know a Dave and Adriana who are regulars here?"

Pablo shrugged and shook his head.

Another waitress and the cook came over then. Justin told them his story. "I need to know who this Dave guy is. He came here a lot with Adriana."

"Who are you?" the cook asked.

"Just a guy who's in Ms. Adriana Sanchez's Algebra class. I'm trying to find out where she is," Justin said.

The cook smiled. "You've come to the right guy. I know that the boyfriend's name is Dave West. He and Adriana eloped to Las Vegas," he said.

Chapter 6

"Are you sure?" Justin asked.

The cook smiled again. "Yep. They were sitting right over there in the corner booth, all lovey-dovey. Then he put a ring on her finger and away they went," he said.

"When was this?" Justin asked.

"Sunday night, around 9:30, I guess. He got real romantic, that dude. He actually picked her up and carried her out to the car. I heard her say 'But what about my classes at the high school?' He laughed and said 'Classes, this is love, baby.'"

Justin wasn't sure what to think. Could he have been all wrong about Ms. Sanchez caring so much about her teaching and the kids? Did she just dump it all and run off with that Dave guy?

"Hey, kid," the cook added with a wink, "I'm sorry if this is bad news for you. Did you have a crush on the lady or something? She's a real beauty all right."

Justin stared at the man, then turned and walked out. He felt totally confused. How could he have been so wrong about the teacher who cared so much that she turned his life around?

Justin was almost to his motorcycle when something caught his eye—the red sports car, the same one he saw at school. The bumper sticker said *I'd rather be loafing*, and that's why Justin recognized it. That was the boyfriend's car all right. But if he and Ms. Sanchez were in Nevada getting married, what was the car doing here?

Justin melted back into the darkness and watched the red car. He waited an hour before the owner appeared. It was the cook from Caleb's, the guy who told Justin about Ms. Sanchez eloping.

"Liar!" Justin hissed under his breath as the man drove away. Justin jumped on his motorcycle and followed him at a distance until he arrived at a fancy townhouse. The guy parked his car and disappeared into the townhouse. Justin cruised by and read the name on the mail box, *D. Jefferies*.

"Yeah," Justin muttered. The Js were torn from Ms. Sanchez's address book. Justin drove directly to the police station and told Lt. Wong what he'd learned. "Well, well, we will have to talk to Mr. Jefferies," the lieutenant promised.

"Have you heard from Ms. Sanchez's parents yet? Do they know anything?" Justin asked.

"They've been contacted, but they couldn't give us anymore information about where their daughter is," Lt.

Wong said.

Justin didn't get home until just before midnight. His parents were furious.

"You've got to stop this crazy obsession with finding Ms. Sanchez," Dad yelled.

"Yes, it could be dangerous," Mom agreed.

"You guys don't understand," Justin said. "I mean, before Ms. Sanchez came along I didn't think I was smart enough to do anything! I owe her something!"

At school the next day, as Justin got off his motorcycle, Dave Jefferies confronted him. "Kid, I got a bone to pick with you. You're Justin Alvarez, right?" he asked. "Well, look, Alvarez, I don't appreciate you turning the cops onto me over this business with my ex-girlfriend doing a vanishing act," Dave snarled.

"You lied about what happened to her," Justin said. "There is no Dave West, and she didn't elope."

"Okay, so I lied. I just wanted to get rid of you, stupid. So I'll lay the truth on you like I told the cops. I just wanted to be friends with Adriana. She wanted marriage. I told her Sunday night to stop pressuring me. She got all hysterical, screamed for me to get out. That's the last I saw of her. I guess she took it so hard she did something desperate."

Chapter 7

"I never saw her lose her cool," Justin said.

"She was crazy about me. She didn't take my *adios* very well. Maybe she took a jet to Paris or who knows?... Now get off my case. I don't need the hassle. She was just a babe to me. Easy come, easy go," Jefferies said.

Justin hated Dave Jefferies. He couldn't imagine Ms. Sanchez even dating such a guy. Maybe he was finally telling the truth about what happened, but Justin still hated him. Maybe if Ms. Sanchez was dumb enough to date such a creep, she was foolish enough to freak out when she lost him. Maybe, but Justin didn't think so. Justin still figured Ms. Sanchez and Dave were casual friends, and suddenly he turned dangerous. She was just getting to know him when she got to know him too well. Something terrible had happened.

The phone was ringing when Justin got home that afternoon.

"You left your name and phone number with my parents," a woman said. "We live next door to Ms. Sanchez's house. My parents feel guilty because when you asked them for information they lied and said they knew nothing."

Justin hurried over to Ms. Sanchez's house and went next door. A tall, thin woman let him in. The woman's parents sat nervously on a nearby couch. "My parents were afraid to get mixed-up in something bad. That's why they didn't tell you. But, you see, Sunday night they heard screams from the driveway of Ms. Sanchez's house. They looked out and someone was forcing her into a car ..."

Justin turned ice cold. "Why didn't they call the police?" he cried.

"Because, you see, it was not so different from how many couples act. They fight and scream. They thought Adriana was having a fight with her boyfriend. They didn't want to get mixed-up in a fight like that. It would have been different if the man was a stranger, but it was the man she was seeing. The man in the red sports car," the woman explained.

Justin told Lt. Wong what the woman told him. "Well, the story Jefferies told us was that they drove off in his car, and they were fighting at the restaurant. Then she took off. So what those people saw sort of ties in with his story."

"But she was screaming. He forced her into his car," Justin insisted.

"That's an interpretation of the situation which may or may not be true," Lt. Wong said. "You can see how a couple might be scrapping and shoving. It would look like a dangerous situation, but it wouldn't be that at all."

Justin climbed on his motorcycle and headed home. He thought back to junior high. He got all Ds and Fs in math and not much better in his other subjects. He had to repeat a year. Now, as a freshman, he was older than most of the other kids. Everybody joked about what a dummy he was. Justin even accepted himself that way. He stopped trying.

He might have never come out of his descent into a nowhere life if Adriana Sanchez hadn't come along and been there for him. She really helped him to do better. He found stuff in himself he never knew he had. Now he was making pretty good grades in everything. He had dreams. She'd given him that.

And maybe she was in terrible trouble. He had to do something to help her. If she voluntarily ditched everything in her sadness over losing Jefferies, then he had to know that for sure. But he couldn't stand for it all to just hang there, a mystery.

Chapter 8

Justin returned to the restaurant at a time when he knew Jefferies wasn't working. He wanted to talk to the waitresses and maybe find out something.

The girls told Justin that Dave was a real charmer one minute and a creep the next. He wasn't somebody you would want to mess with. One waitress told Justin in a whisper, "He's loaded with money. Nobody knows where it comes from. I mean, he's a fry cook, right? You don't get rich being a fry cook in a place like this, right?"

"What do you think?" Justin asked.

"Well, listen, don't quote me. He's got something going on at a warehouse over on 14th Street. It's a big deserted